ALI
THE
GREAT
and the Market Mishap

by SAADIA FARUQI   illustrated by DEBBY RAHMALIA

PICTURE WINDOW BOOKS
a capstone imprint

D1414045

FoR AdaM —SF
FoR ALesha —DR

Published by Picture Window Books, an imprint of Capstone
1710 Roe Crest Drive
North Mankato, Minnesota 56003
capstonepub.com

Library of Congress Cataloging-in-Publication Data:
Names: Faruqi, Saadia, author. | Rahmalia, Debby, illustrator.
Title: Ali the Great and the market mishap / written by Saadia Faruqi;
illustrated by Debby Rahmalia.
Description: North Mankato, Minnesota : Picture Window Books, an
imprint of Capstone, 2023. | Series: Ali the Great | Audience: Ages
5 to 8 | Audience: Grades K-1 | Summary: Second-grader Ali, his
grandfather, and little brother Fateh head to the South Asian market
to buy some snacks, but Ali loses Fateh and has to figure out quickly
how to find him among the market's many aisles.
Identifiers: LCCN 2022048875 (print) | LCCN 2022048876 (ebook) |
  ISBN 9781666393873 (hardcover) | ISBN 9781484681138 (paperback)
  ISBN 9781484681145 (pdf) | ISBN 9781484687567 (kindle edition) |
  ISBN 9781484681169 (epub)
Subjects: LCSH: Pakistani Americans—Juvenile fiction. | Brothers—
Juvenile fiction. | Ethnic markets—Juvenile fiction. | Missing children—
Juvenile fiction. | CYAC: Pakistani Americans—Fiction. | Brothers—
Fiction. | Ethnic markets—Fiction. | Missing children—Fiction.
Classification: LCC PZ7.1.F373 Ali 2023 (print) | LCC PZ7.1.F373
(ebook) | DDC [E]—dc23
LC record available at https://lccn.loc.gov/2022048875
LC ebook record available at https://lccn.loc.gov/2022048876

Designers: Kay Fraser and Tracy Davies

TABLE OF CONTENTS

I'M ALI TAHIR, aLSO KNOWN AS

ALI
THE
GREAT!

And this is My FaMiLy...

ABBA
doctor

AMMA
scientist

DADA
chief joke teller

DADI
best cook in
the WoRLd

FATEH
sneaky LittLe bRotHer

LET'S LEARN SOME URDU!

Ali and his family speak both English and Urdu, a language from Pakistan. Now you'll know some Urdu too!

ABBA (ah-BAH)—father (also baba)

AMMA (ah-MAH)—mother (also mama)

BHAI (BHA-ee)—brother

DADA (DAH-dah)—grandfather on father's side

DADI (DAH-dee)—grandmother on father's side

SALAAM (sah-LAHM)—hello

SHUKRIYA (shuh-KREE-yuh)—thank you

Chapter 1

WE NEED SNACKS

The rain had finally stopped.

"I'm all out of snacks," Dada announced.

Dada was Ali's favorite person. Dada and Dadi, Ali's grandparents, lived with his family.

Ali grinned. "A growing boy
needs snacks too!" He loved
crackers with cheese. And tiny
pizza rolls. And cookies!

But Dada loved Pakistani
snacks, because that's where he
was from.

Dada snapped his fingers. "How about a trip to the market?" he said.

"Hooray!" Going out with Dada was always fun.

Ali grabbed his shoes. Dada helped Ali's little brother, Fateh, into his stroller.

"You better not get in any trouble, mister!" Dada teased Fateh.

Fateh just laughed. One thing Fateh was good at was trouble.

"I'll keep an eye on him,
Dada!" Ali said proudly. "That's
what big brothers do."

They walked on the sidewalk.
At least, *Dada* walked. Fateh
wiggled in his stroller. Ali jumped
over puddles as he counted them.

"Ten!" Ali shouted.

"Careful, Ali!" Dada warned.

Ali grinned. "I'm always
careful!"

Chapter 2

THE MARKET

The South Asian market was very big.

They headed inside and left Fateh's stroller at the front. Ali loved the market. He looked around in awe.

"Amazing . . . ," Ali whispered.

They passed the vegetable carts

and the frozen foods section. Ali

saw lots of cold soda bottles and

huge bags of rice. There was even

a section of colorful toys.

"Keep an eye on your brother—and look for those chips I like, please," Dada said as they reached the snack area. Then he continued down the aisle to find the things on his list.

"Uh-huh," said Ali.

There were hundreds of snacks on the shelves. Crispy nimko. Sweet and spicy candy. Salty chickpeas.

Then Ali saw a big display of spicy chips.

"Gimme!" Fateh shouted.

Oops, thought Ali. Fateh loved chips, just like Dada.

"You can't have these, buddy," he said. "Too spicy."

Fateh didn't listen. He let go of Ali's hand and ran straight at the display.

Ali leaped forward and grabbed the cardboard display before it tipped over.

Phew! Those were some cool moves!

"Thank you very much!" Ali said and took a bow, even though nobody was around.

Wait, where was Fateh?

☆ Chapter 3 ☆
THE RESCUE

Ali knew he had to find his little brother, fast! He ran down the snack aisle, past a store clerk. No Fateh.

He went to the front of the store and looked inside the stroller.

Sometimes Fateh liked to hide in there. Nope.

"Fateh!" Ali whispered loudly. "Where are you?"

There was no reply. Ali gulped. This was bad. Very, very bad. Dada would be so mad that Ali had lost his little brother.

Then Ali saw a ladder.

Yes! He got a brilliant idea. He climbed up the ladder and craned his neck. From up high, Ali could see the whole store! He looked so hard his eyes hurt.

"Hey—be careful!" a store clerk called out.

Just then, Ali saw Fateh's red
shirt in the toy section. He jumped
down and ran through the aisles.

There was Fateh, sitting
between two shelves. "Come here,
silly goose!" Ali said and reached
for him.

"No!" Fateh yelled.

Ali looked around and saw

the spicy chips. He grabbed one

and dangled it in front of Fateh.

"Come get it!"

Fateh's eyes grew big.

"Gimme!" he said and toddled

toward Ali.

"Gotcha!" Ali picked up his brother and held him close. "No more exploring for you."

They met Dada at the checkout counter.

"Ah, Fateh found the spicy chips for us!" Dada said and put the bag in his cart.

Ali nodded. "Oh yes, he was a *big* help," he said.

Fateh smiled.

JUST JOKING AROUND

How does a hen measure her eggs?
Egg-zactly

Waiter: Do you want dessert, sir?
Teddy Bear: No, thanks. I'm stuffed.

What do you call a sad strawberry?
A blue berry

SNACK TIME!

Dada loves snacks from his home country of Pakistan. Here are some of his favorites:

crispy nimko: a delicious mix of chips, nuts, and crispy noodles

kulfi: frozen dessert made with evaporated milk

salty chickpeas: chickpeas roasted with salt, red chili powder, and other spices

spicy chips: crispy chips with spicy flavor

sweet and spicy candy: multicolored gummy bears mixed with spices

THINK BIG WITH

ALI THE GREAT!

⭐ Have you ever been lost in a store? What did you do? How do you think Ali handled the situation when his brother was lost?

⭐ Write another chapter to this story. What happens on the way home from the market?

⭐ What are your favorite snacks? Can you think of foods you like for each color of the rainbow? Draw them!

☆ About the Author ☆

Saadia Faruqi is a Pakistani American writer, interfaith activist, and cultural sensitivity trainer featured in *O, The Oprah Magazine*. Author of the Yasmin chapter book series, Saadia also writes middle grade novels, such as *Yusuf Azeem Is Not a Hero*, and other books for children. Saadia is editor-in-chief of *Blue Minaret*, an online magazine of poetry, short stories, and art. Besides writing, she also loves reading, binge-watching her favorite shows, and taking naps. She lives in Houston with her family.

☆ About the Illustrator ☆

Debby Rahmalia is an illustrator based in Indonesia with a passion for storytelling. She enjoys creating diverse works that showcase an array of cultures and people. Debby's long-term dream was to become an illustrator. She was encouraged to pursue her dream after she had her first baby and has been illustrating ever since. When she's not drawing, she spends her time reading the books she illustrated to her daughter or wandering around the neighborhood with her.

JOIN ALI THE GREAT ON His Adventures!

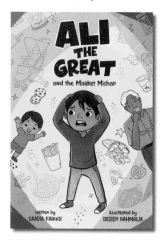

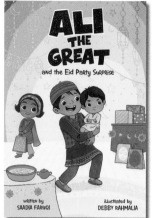